DC Super Hero Girls™

WEIRD SCIENCE

written by
AMANDA DEIBERT

art by
**YANCEY LABAT, ERICH OWEN,
MARCELO DiCHIARA, AGNES GARBOWSKA,
SARAH LEUVER, AND EMMA KUBERT**

colored by **CARRIE STRACHAN, ERICH OWEN,
WENDY BROOME, SILVANA BRYS, SARAH LEUVER,
AND EMMA KUBERT**

lettering by **JANICE CHIANG**

SUPERGIRL based on the
characters created by
JERRY SIEGEL and JOE SHUSTER.
By special arrangement with
the JERRY SIEGEL FAMILY.

DC Super Hero Girls™

WEIRD SCIENCE

KRISTY QUINN Editor
STEVE COOK Design Director - Books
AMIE BROCKWAY-METCALF Publication Design

BOB HARRAS Senior VP - Editor-in-Chief, DC Comics
MICHELE R. WELLS VP & Executive Editor, Young Reader

DAN DiDIO Publisher
JIM LEE Publisher & Chief Creative Officer
BOBBIE CHASE VP - New Publishing Initiatives
DON FALLETTI VP - Manufacturing Operations & Workflow Management
LAWRENCE GANEM VP - Talent Services
ALISON GILL Senior VP - Manufacturing & Operations
HANK KANALZ Senior VP - Publishing Strategy & Support Services
DAN MIRON VP - Publishing Operations
NICK J. NAPOLITANO VP - Manufacturing Administration & Design
NANCY SPEARS VP - Sales
JONAH WEILAND VP - Marketing & Creative Services

DC Super Hero Girls: Weird Science
Published by DC Comics.

Printed at LSC Communications, Crawfordsville, IN, USA. 6/5/2020. First Printing.

DC - a WarnerMedia Company

DC Comics, 2900 West Alameda Ave., Burbank, CA 91505

ISBN: 978-1-4012-9846-3

Library of Congress Cataloging-in-Publication Data

Names: Deibert, Amanda, author. | Labat, Yancey C., illustrator. | Strachan, Carrie, colourist. | Chiang, Janice, letterer.
Title: Weird science / written by Amanda Deibert ; illustrated by Yancey Labat [and five others] ; colored by Carrie Strachan [and five others] ; lettering by Janice Chiang.
Description: Burbank, CA : DC Comics, [2020] | Series: DC super hero girls | "Supergirl based on the characters created by Jerry Siegel and Joe Shuster." | Audience: Grades 4-6. | Summary: "It's science fair time at Metropolis High, and the DC Super Hero Girls are very excited-except for Zee Zatara. Magic is her life, and science seems so dull in comparison. When she tries to help her friends with their projects, things keep going wrong. Is her magic causing the science to go haywire? Actually, science is just like being part of a superhero team: when you combine the right ingredients, it's magic"-- Provided by publisher.
Identifiers: LCCN 2020012881 (print) | LCCN 2020012882 (ebook) | ISBN 9781401298463 (paperback) | ISBN 9781779504838 (ebook)
Subjects: LCSH: Graphic novels. | CYAC: Graphic novels. | Science projects--Fiction. | Magic--Fiction. | Superheroes--Fiction. | High schools--Fiction. | Schools--Fiction.
Classification: LCC PZ7.7.D4467 2020 (print) | LCC PZ7.7.D4467 (ebook) | DDC 741.5/973--dc23
LC record available at https://lccn.loc.gov/2020012881
LC ebook record available at https://lccn.loc.gov/2020012882

chapter one

drawn by Yancey Labat,
colored by Carrie Strachan

Oh em gee, I'm saving lives **and** using my batarangs!
Best Monday evaaar!
Do you like ice cream? Because if you are willing to just walk away right now, we could share an amazing vegan cone.
THE DAILY PLANET
SNAP!
SIZZLE!
Giganta, we will not be intimidated. I've fought gods much larger than you.

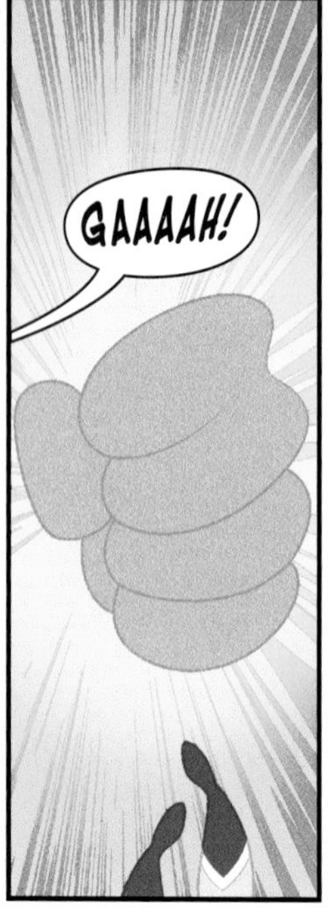

Excuse me. Sorry.
Bumblebee, did you just apologize for fighting the villain?
Sorry.

She's so **huge!**
I mean, have you ever seen anything like her?

Oh, you haven't seen anything yet.

I've got her, Zatanna.
Thanks, Wonder Woman. I'll take it from here.

Ladies and gentlemen, it's time for the main event. Watch as I make all your problems disappear!
Llihc tuo!

-Gasp!- She vanished into thin air!
Zatanna is amazing! Hooray!

Zatanna, where did you send her, exactly?
Oh, just somewhere to chill. She's, like, across town or something I think.

Z-Z-Z-Z-A-A-A-T-A-N-N-A, I'LL G-G-GET YOU.

Oh, bats! We gotta get to school.
BUZZ!
BUZZ!
BUZZ!

Wait!
I am not about to let my dearest friends walk into Metropolis High looking like a bunch of hot messes.
What's up, Zee?

Students, today I have a *very* exciting announcement.
This year's annual science fair will be handled a bit differently.
We have a special guest judge from the Project Cadmus.

Groan.
Ugh.
Science?!
Eeeeeeee, Karen! A real scientist from the actual Project Cadmus.
Ohmigosh, Babs! I had no idea when they called us in here it would be for something so totally exciting!

Please welcome Dr. Penelope Sieve.
Thank you so much for having me, Principal Chapin.
Students of Metropolis High, I'm looking forward to your projects!
And I'm pleased to announce that the prize for this year's winning entry will be a summer internship with Cadmus—

AHHHHHH!
EEEEEEEEEE!!!

In addition, the charming local café Sweet Justice has agreed to sponsor our fair and is offering the winner a year of unlimited goodies!

Yes!

Oh, um...
Yes, Ms.—?
Hi, I'm um, Karen Beecher. I was just wondering if there are any parameters for the projects?

I can tell you're one to keep my eye on. My only parameter is the one rule we have at Cadmus: take risks.
If you can't fail spectacularly, it's not worth doing.

That's **my** philosophy exactly.
She's amaaaazing.

Yes?
Is science fair participation required?
I'll take this one. Yes, Ms. Zatara. Due to the incredible opportunity, all teachers in the science department have agreed it will make up eighty percent of your final grade, no matter which science class you're enrolled in.

I've gotta say, meeting up at Sweet Justice after school is going to be sooooo much more fun after I get that sweet, sweet prize!
Sweet JUSTICE
SHAKES MALTS
Sweet JUSTICE
COOKIES
I love the confident approach. You will be a worthy opponent in this battle for science.
It's on!

I was thinking I would ask that student I met from the military school, Steve, to help me work on a demonstration on the physics of proper self-defense.
Oh em gee, you two have **such** chemistry!

No, our project will be physics. Not chemistry.

What about you, Karen?
I was thinking about tracking the flight patterns of honeybees, from the never-before-seen vantage point of a tiny camera mounted to a bee.
Just any old bee?

Well, that's what I'll tell Dr. Sieve. Wait... do you think that's cheating?
Absolutely **not.** Girl, you gotta just **bee** yourself.
Hahaha, wow, I am hilarious sometimes.

Okay, so what I am going to do is build a robot sidekick!
A robot to kick your sides?

No, I mean a sidekick. If Batman can have a Robin then why can't Batgirl have a...

SPARROW!

I'll give you credit, Babs, that is a pretty flashy idea.
What about you, Zee?

Yeah, you've been really quiet. Which is...weird. Are you sick? I can totally fly out and get you some soup.
I'm fine, I just...look, I know you and Babs love science, but honestly, I find the whole thing boring.

Besides, I use magic all the time, so it's not like I need to learn about this stuff anyway.

Science can totally feel like magic, I promise. Why don't you come with me tomorrow? I'll show you!
Yeah, and then come with me to Smallville!

You can help us *all* with our projects, at least until you figure something out.
Yes, count me in, my friend. There's got to be something science related you will enjoy.
As much as I enjoy this?

You are truly spectacular, Zee.
I know.

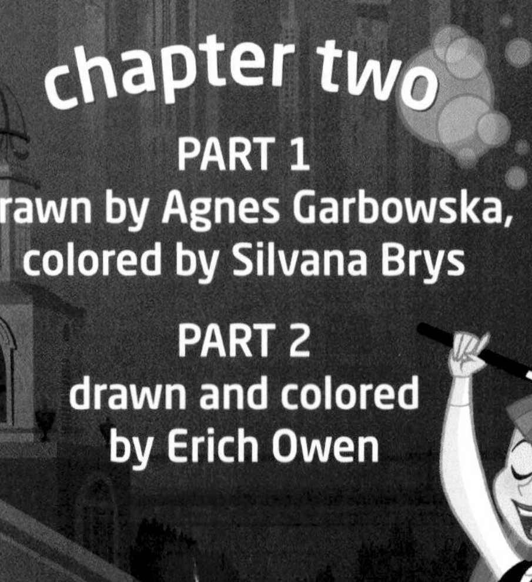

chapter two

PART 1
drawn by Agnes Garbowska,
colored by Silvana Brys

PART 2
drawn and colored
by Erich Owen

Ready to film some bees?
Wow, it is ***gorgeous*** here.

It's the ***perfect*** backdrop for a frielfie!
"Frielfie"?

Selfie with a friend. Obvs!
Say "BEES!"
Oh...

ZeeZatara
KarenBeecher
ZeeZatara
ZeeZatara #Flowerchild #NaturalHabitat #BestBees #ZeesBees #KarenIsSharin
Okay. I'll shrink down and you can take notes.
No way am I missing out on the action.

Ylfrettub!
POOF!
Ta-da!
You look perfect. But, um, just a reminder, please try to avoid getting caught on my antenna cam.
As much as it pains me, I promise to stay out of the spotlight...
•REC

Look! Bombus pennsylvanicus!

Did you just use a spell?! I thought this whole experiment was anti-magic?
Oh sorry, no. Ha ha. I use scientific names when I'm excited.
Antenna
Head
Fore wing
Thorax

I will say all this nature stuff is pretty rela—Aaaa AAAA-choooo!

Whoops, excuse me.
Whoa, Zatanna, your wings!

Uh, Bumblebee—
I think the sudden burst of magic startled him. Just be still for a moment.

Doooon't move...
This is one of the creepiest experiences of my life...and that's saying a lot.

Whew!
See? Bees are fine with butterflies. It's just a good thing you didn't choose to become some kind of predator.

Okay, time to head into the hive. Take this so you aren't arriving empty-handed...er, legged.
I do love a good hostess gift!

Thank you, I'll just—AA-Aah

CHOOOOO!
POOF!

W-w-where am I?

This is gonna be a long flight home.

Eebelbmub nruter!

I'M SOOOO SORRY. I THINK I MIGHT BE ALLERGIC TO NATURE.
ON THE BRIGHT SIDE, I'VE LEARNED MY SUIT CAN WITHSTAND SUB-ZERO TEMPERATURES.

WAIT...DOES EVERYONE YOU MAKE DISAPPEAR GO TO THE SAME PLACE? SHOULD WE BE WORRIED ABOUT GIGANTA?
OH NO, THAT WAS INTENTIONAL. YOURS WAS AN ACCIDENT. I'M SURE IT'S FINE.

INCREDIBLE.
WOW, I WONDER IF I COULD GET DAD TO DESIGN A BACKDROP LIKE THIS FOR OUR SHOW.

THIS FOOTAGE IS GOING TO BE SO GREAT!
•REC

What are they doing?
WHRRRRR
BUZZZZZ
WHRRRRRR
•REC

They flap their wings to help the water evaporate...it makes the honey thicker and stickier.
WHRRRRR
WHRRRR
BUZZZZ
It also makes the pollen fly into the air and A-AAAA-AAA
Oh no! Oh no!

CHOOOO!

Um, Zatanna...
I know, I know. It's a bit too goth.

BUZZ!
BUZZ!
BUZZ!
We have bigger concerns than fashion.
For once, I'm going to agree.

Ah!

Bumblebee!

BUZZ!
BUZZ!
Ooof!

I'M stuck, too!
I'll just transform us back to our normal size!
NO!

No?
It'll destroy the hive and then I won't have a school project.

Besides, do you wanna be the one to tell Jessica we destroyed a creature's habitat?
Good point.
Okay, I'll try this.
Ylfrettub!

Maybe they'll calm down.

BUZZ!
BUZZ!
BUZZ!
Or not.

Smoke!
What?
Beekeepers use smoke to calm bees. Could you conjure some?

Ekoms Wohs!

That should have worked! Why isn't it working?!
BUZZ!
BUZZ!
We'd better think of something fast, or we are toast. And I mean smeared on toast in a dollop of honey!
BUZZ

BUZZ!
BUZZ!
BUZZ!
Ooof!
Ugh!
BUZZ!
Zzub ffo!
BUZZ!
I don't get it. Your smoke should have worked, Zatanna. I guess they're just really focused on protecting their queen.
BUZZ!
I'm sorry! I don't want to hurt you! *Please* stop attacking us.
BUZZ!
BUZZ!
BUZZ!
BUZZ!

Help me out of this goo, Bumblebee. I think I have an idea.
Just please not anything that will destroy the hive.
BUZZ!
BUZZ!
BUZZ!
It won't, I promise.
Eeb neeuq!
Royal problems deserve a royal solution.
POOF!

ZZZZZ
ZZZZZ
ZZZZZ
ZZZZZ
ZZZZZ
ZZZZZ
Bee-hold your new queen!
Queen bees don't wear crowns.
This queen bee does.
Now leave us be.
Whoa, it worked!
Sometimes all it takes is a little pizzazz. Let's finish your project.

Wait, where's my camera? And my antenna?

They've gotta be in here somewhere.

This is no work for a queen.

Oh, loyal subjects.

You know, I was wrong. Being a bee is **awesome.**
SKRZZZZ
I mean, I enjoy it. But, I don't know...

Magically forcing them to ruin their hive feels wrong.
SKRZZZ
As soon as we find your camera we can get awesome footage of them putting it back together. You'll thank me.
SKRZZZ
SKRZZZ

I guess...

Everything is gonna be just fine...

OUCH!

Hey, that's no way to treat your queen!

Uh, Zatanna, I think that's the real queen.

Only *one* of us is wearing the crown.
Heh-heh...

Your majesty, we don't mean to offend. Please!

Just let my friend...

TRIP!

Go in peace... Ahh!
BUMP!

Wow. You know, you didn't have to do that.
Oh no! Oh gosh, I'm sorry. I can't believe I just did.

BUZZ!
BUZZ!
BUZZ!
I can fight my own battles.
A hive can't have two queens. She's not going to stop fighting...

That's fine. I always win my fights.
BUZZ!
BUZZ!
It's a fight to the death.
BUZZ!

BUZZ!
BUZZ!
What are we going to do?!

I'll get us to the exit.

You won't be able to carry me!

I won't have to.

AHHHHHH!!!
ZATANNA!
Erotser!
THUMP
Pant! Pant! Pant!

Head for the water!

Elbbub sdaeh!
SPLASH

I guess we know biology isn't my jam. I'm really sorry about your suit, Bumblebee.
Oh, that's okay. I'm sure I can fix it and still have time to do my project!

Well, if you need any help...
Oh, I'll be fine. You can go ahead and help Kara with her project.

chapter three

drawn by Yancey Labat,
colored by Carrie Strachan

Welcome to
SMALLVILLE
Wow, this is a much prettier view than I ever had riding in on the tour bus with Dad.

Good morning!

Supergirl?!

Tolipotua!

Now *that's* making an entrance.

Kara!

This is my friend Zatanna. When she's incognito, it's Zee.
Nice to meet you, Zee.
Thanks for the lemonade, Mrs. Kent.

So, my big science project is gonna be to help you make the farm run more efficiently now that you don't have my help.
That's very sweet, Kara. I'll leave you girls to it.

Sooo...this is what farm life is like, huh?
Yep.

I totally get why you got yourself kicked out of school to get out of here.
I didn't! I mean—I love life in Metropolis, but I was framed!
I'm just saying I wouldn't blame you.

Let's test her out.

When I say go, you turn it on and we'll see which of us harvests faster.
GO!

Hey! Not bad! We've got it almost as quick as me.
Hooray...can we take a break now? There's got to be **something** fun to do around here.

In Smallville?
Oh come on, surely you have parties in a barn or something? **Puh-lease?**
Sigh.

Welcome to Smallville.
Oh wow, I was kidding about the barn.
Now *this* is more like it.
Turnip the beet, turnip the beet, YEAH!
Turnip the beet...

Yeah! Turnip the beet!

HEY!

AHHHHHHHHHHH!
Sorry!

This is *exactly* why she got kicked out of Smallville High.
Lucky for us all. What a freak.

You heard them?
The downside of super-hearing.

Time for a show.

Here, lemme give you a hand.

Whoa, look at you—making it rain!
How did you do that?

WHAT?!
What can I say? I've always had a green thumb.

I saw you on tour with your dad last year.

Your style is so incredible. Does everyone in the city dress like this?

Well, I mean, ***obviously*** I am devastatingly cool with impeccable style...but you know who really reigns supreme over at Metropolis High?

Your girl Kara here is the coolest.

Kara, the horror?
Horror if you aren't in her clique, sure.

Oh yeah, that edgy punk vibe is *totally* the rage in Metropolis. Gosh, I bet you were all fighting to make her your prom queen when she was here.

Come on, Kara. Let's find a place with a cooler vibe.

Bye, Kara! Don't forget to write to your B.F.F.s!
Come back soon... and bring your friend Zee. And some clothes we can borrow!
Yeah, we always *really* liked you.

You totally didn't have to do that...but thanks.
Anytime.

Did we leave the tractor running?
Absolutely not.

Oh no! We've gotta stop it!
BWAAK!

Okay, girl of steel, it's time to get metal.

ZOOM!

Okay, I know I said Smallville was lacking in excitement...

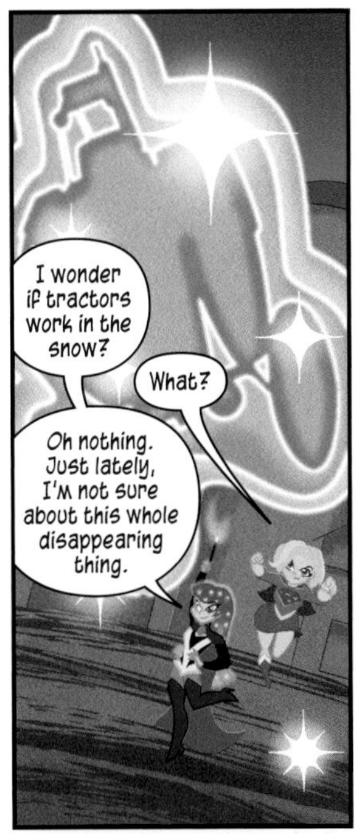
I wonder if tractors work in the snow?
What?
Oh nothing. Just lately, I'm not sure about this whole disappearing thing.

Do you think magic set these things off?
Certainly not any of mine!

Okay, that was maybe not my best idea.
SMASH!

Whoa! Cold.

Whoops! I didn't mean that so literally.

We've got to get this cleaned up before the Kents see it.

How's it going, girls? Oh my...

I know it looks bad, Ma, but I promise we can fix it.

Skcud!

Look! Now you have a pond!

I'll just go inside and call Clark to come help you girls.
QUACK!

No! I mean, it's totally not necessary. We've got it under control.

Supergirl is right.
I know it looks bad, but as a magician I can assure you that looks can be deceiving.
Just give us until tomorrow. It'll be better than new.
Okay, Kara. Okay.

I can't have Clark come fix my mistakes. This whole thing is supposed to be about proving how I can be just as big a help as Superman.
You still can be! It's just one setback.

Erotser!

See? Good as new. Wanna try again?
I'm not touching those machines. But Karen helped me create some quick-growing fertilizer. The old science project is over!

Long live the new, stronger science project!
It certainly *smells* stronger.

It'll be so helpful when it only takes half the time for the crops to grow and I can just track **that** for my science project!
Supergirl saves the day!

Um, Supergirl...how quickly is it supposed to grow?
A normal crop takes sixty to a hundred days so probably like a month. Why?

That was **not** supposed to happen.

Zatanna!
Supergirl?! Where are you?

What was *in* this stuff?!

Nrocpop!

What was *in* that fertilizer?
It was supposed to just be cow pats and minerals.

I'm never eating popcorn again.
Hate to break it to you, but that's how *all* your food is grown.

Ugh! That was worse than a fight with Poison Ivy.

At least Ivy never uses manure.

Sigh. I guess I better get rid of that fertilizer.
QUACK.

Hey! Where'd it go?
I don't know.

Maybe when you were making the corn disappear...?
I only made popcorn.

Shall we try again? Third time's the charm!
Actually, I think I'm better off solo. Maybe you should just head back to Metropolis and help Diana.

Oh. Okay. See you Monday...
Sure.

Emoh!

Clark, dear, how are you?! We have a little, uh, situation we could use your help with.
I hate super-hearing. Sigh.

chapter four

drawn by Marcelo DiChiara,
colored by Wendy Broome

METROPOLIS HIGH SCHOOL

Ahhh!

Steve, do you think this color is too raspberry?

Wow, Diana, how did you do that?

Oh, uh...

It's all about understanding your center of gravity.
Yrrebnarc!

So much better.
What should I do first?

I...uh...

Yes?

Sorry, I just had a moment where a feline grabbed my tongue muscles.
What?!
The cat's got her tongue.

Oh...that happens to me a lot, especially right now.
Right. Less talking, more centrifugal force.

Whoa!
Click

Perfection.

Are you getting proper photo documentation for my display?
Oh totally.

This is going to be the best trifold display ever! I think I've finally found science that appeals to me.

After we do a few more, you wanna grab a bite somewhere?

I eat full meals. Not bites.

Oh, okay? I guess we should keep going.
Yes! I enjoy you...er, I mean, doing this project with you.

I enjoy doing this with you, too.
Good. I am glad you like being thrown.

Can I just...will you please accompany me to the ladies room for a sec?

Okay.

No, no! Leave that there!

We'll be back in a flash.

He's here?

You do not need to use the facilities?

Steve has a crush on you.

Okay, first of all he was asking you to go see the movie with him.
Why didn't he just **say** that?

He did. It's just subtle. Here, I'll be Steve.

Evets!

This seems excessive.
It's the Zatara family rule—always dress for the occasion.
So, Diana, it's me, Steve. Do you have plans this weekend?
Yes.

No. If he asks you that you need to say no.
But I am a planner. I **always** have plans!

Listen to me—
if he asks about plans
it means he wants to
go on a date...
with you.
Always?
Always.

If he asks you to
"hang out" you don't ask
"from what?" If he mentions
a movie say, "I'd love to see
it." And if he mentions food in
any capacity, small bites
or large, just go
with him.
Oh...
okay. This
seems like a
lot to
remember.

Just let him
know you don't have plans
and you'd love to do something
with him and you'll be golden.
But first, we've gotta
adjust your look.
My look?

Like I said,
dress for the
occasion.
Srats!

HMMM...too retro?
Stnap!
Eh, too casual.
Dom!
Uh, Zee... this feels...very unlike me.
Yeah, it's a bit of a detour. Oh, I know!
Noitcefrep!

This is the longest restroom break *ever.*

Oh hey, Zee. Where's—

Diana?

Hi, Steve. *Hehehe*...Are you ready to try again?
Um, I g-guess so?

Is dressing like Zee part of the project?

I...yes, I think so? I was trying to slide into comfort?
Slip into something more comfortable.
Yes, that.

Oh, uh, okay... Should we—get back to the science project?
Sure, whatever you say is great!

But it's your project. You should be the one in charge...

Yes, right, I am the leader here. Let's get back to work.

Oh...unless you want to bite food?
Bite food?

I like small and large bites of food. And also your smile!

Thank you, I think? You have a great smile, too.

Really? You think so?
Ow.

Oh my Hera, I am so sorry!
It's fine. Maybe we should just take a break and work on it some more over the weekend.

!?
This weekend? Oh no, I do NOT have any plans to go to the movies with you this weekend.
Huh?

So close.

Maybe we could eat some small bites while we work on defensive maneuvers?

That sounds... like a choking hazard.

Oh, maybe you should tell me what activities we can do and then my eyelashes will turn into bats?
That sounds... really...great. But I just remembered I have to get back to the military academy. I have a ton of homework and lots of extra, uh, marching practice?

Is this playing too rigid to be easily obtained?
He's gonna be hard to get all right...but I don't think he's playing. Sorry. Time to teach you another time-honored tradition of flirting.

Grief milkshakes.

We got your text. What's up?
I'm so glad you're all here. Will someone please order me another milkshake. Extra chocolate?
Whoa. This is serious.

Uh, Diana, why are you dressed like Zee?
An experiment in love. It failed.

Yeah, Zee seems to have a real knack for helping!
What's *that* supposed to mean, Kara?

I'm not trying to be mean. I appreciate all the help with my friends back in Smallville, but also...the farm didn't wreck itself.
I had nothing to do with that!

Karen, you don't think I ruined your project, do you?

Oh, uh, noooo...I mean, maybe, **possibly** there was a little magic happening with the bees, but totally **not** your fault and my project is totally not ruined.
So it's fine.
I'm fine.
Everything is fine.

Wow. I'm gonna just...go for a walk.

So...anyone wanna hear about my robot, Sparrow? She's pretty amazing! If I do say so myself, and I do!

You can still help me with my solar panels tomorrow.
Sure.

Okay, so the thing is, Sparrow is already like a trillion times better than Robin because she's actually strong. Plus, she has a way cooler name.
Batman is gonna be sooooo impressed! Squeee!

Oh, excuse me, Dr. Sieve.
Well, hello! I recognize you! The student who was so reluctant to participate in the science fair. What was your name again?

Zee Zatara.
Zatara, right. So, have you had any luck coming up with a project worthy of your time?

To be honest, the only thing I've managed to accomplish is finding out how many science projects I can ruin.
Hahaha! Oh, it can't be that bad!

Walk with me for a moment. I want to tell you a story.

When I first started, I wasn't even sure I liked science.
Really?
Really.

"Everyone else seemed so naturally gifted in the lab and I couldn't keep up. So I worked alone.

"And in doing so I created a tragedy.

"I lost my work...and almost lost my life.
KA-BOOM!

"After that, I decided to work with—and learn from—those who were smarter than me.

And thanks to their help, guess who now has more patents than any other scientist at Project Cadmus?

It's just...
Don't worry. I'm not saying you ***have*** to become a scientist.

I'm just saying it's good to step back and realize when you ***aren't*** the most talented person in the room...however rare that may be.
CANDY
COOKIES
MENU

And then let those around you help you grow and become even more amazing.

Thank you so much, Dr. Sieve. You're right. I might actually need to step out of the spotlight... I mean, just for a moment.

PART 1
drawn and colored
by Erich Owen

PART 2
drawn and colored
by Sarah Leuver

Thanks for meeting me up here, Zee.
The view is stellar. I'm ***for sure*** using this in a photo shoot later.

Just these few panels should be able to power the entire school. The key is finding a spot that gets plenty of sunlight throughout the day.

That's odd...

The forecast didn't say anything about rain. I think something might be wrong.

It does feel little shady to me.
I'm not usually a fan of puns. But that was pretty good.

I'm always ready to entertain.

There's no way my solar project is going to work as long as the sun is hidden. Wanna head downtown and help me walk some shelter dogs?

In this darkness? We won't be able to see to walk anywhere.

Besides—we won't be defeated that easily.

Well, it's not quite the brightest day...I guess we could use some of Green Lantern's light.

Enihs!
That is **not** what I meant to do.
Well, at least it's pretty?
Maybe a little wind energy will help?
I don't understand why nothing is working.

BZZZZ
BZZZZ

Okay, either Catwoman is currently ravaging the city with a bunch of feral cats... or Diana has adopted some new pets.

Oh, I hope it is kitty adoptions! There are so many animals who need homes. And that's why it's so important to spay and neuter!
Uh, great. We should...probably go help her save the city.

How are we supposed to stop criminals when we can't even see them?

Batgirl!?

Zatanna, Green Lantern! Down here!

MEOW!
MEOW!
MEOW!

MEOW!
MEOW!
MEOW!
MEOW!

Why do you have the Bat-signal in an alley?
It's the only way we can see all the cats!
Where is everyone else?
TWANG!
MEOW!
MEOW!
RRRRRRR!!!
MEOW!
CRASH!
MEOW!

Show yourself, Catwoman! We know you're behind this.

HA HA HA! It's a shame only one of us can see in the dark.

THWANG!

THWANG!

Help me! Help me! AAA...AAA!

What's happening? Are you being attacked? Did Catwoman scratch you??
Oh no, I just have a terrible allergy to ca— ⇒AAA-aaachoooo!⇐

I got this. I'll drop her off across town and be right back.

Oh! ⇒Achoo!⇐ You are such a sweet young lady.
Please don't tell anyone.

Okay, enough of this chaos, Catwoman. You've had your fun.
Ahhhhh. Shoo, kitties! Shoo!

Oh, I'm just getting started! Usually my feline friends and I have to wait until dark, but now is our time to finally shine.
You know what they say—"While the sun's away, the cats will play."

Um, I'm pretty sure that's not how the saying goes...
It is now. As long as this eclipse lasts, the city is mine.
HISsssss

Ereh, yttik, yttik!

Come with us peacefully and we will not harm you.
But my friends are going to harm you.
HISSSSSSS!
Allow me.
Eeeek, we are totally capturing Catwoman! This is the best day ever!

MEOW!
HISS!
RAWWWRRR!
How are there so many cats?!
See...this is exactly what I was saying about spaying and neutering.
My hair!
I'm back. Let's take these cats to the pound...or at least start pounding!
No, you mustn't hurt them. It's not their fault.

Here ya go...follow the laser light.
MEOW.
MEW.

ANIMAL SHELT
We're just going to let Catwoman get away?

Oh, not at all.

Great work, team, but we need to be diligent. As long as it stays this dark we can expect more crime.
Then we better figure out how to shed a little light on a solution.
Hahahaha! Shed some light. I love it.

I'm trying not to take it personally, but these clouds appeared as soon as I set up the solar panels.

According to my Bat-Doppler, it was supposed to be sunny.

Ohhhh, centrifugal force.
My blood-pumping internal organ may be broken after sparring with Steve, but the lessons from my project are still useful.

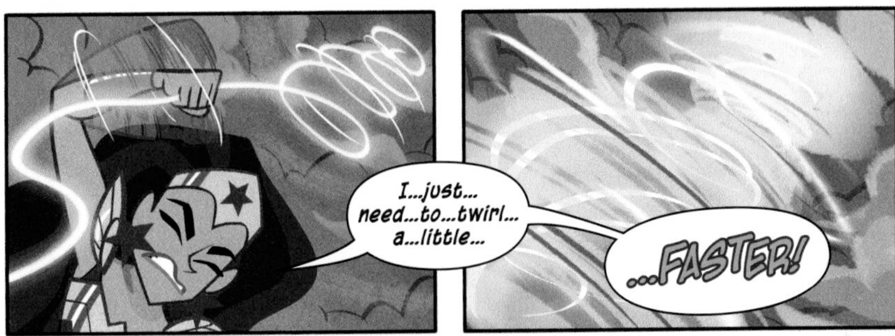
I...just... need...to...twirl... a...little...
...FASTER!

I feel like I am on a round circle of merriment!
A what?
I think she means merry-go-round?
Whatever she means, we should probably stop the ride before she hurls.

Um, Supergirl, do you need some help?
I've got her... Ooof!

Rohcna pord!

I cannot believe that did not work.
Well, at least we have a little sun now.

I've got an idea!

WHOOOSH!

Awww, look, Batgirl, one looks like a kitten!
Too soon, Bumblebee. Too soon.

This is impossible!

Okay, Supergirl, don't get mad, but...I made a gadget that might work a little bit better...
And it's super cool!

Ta-da!
Seriously? Bat-breath?

Ohhh—
great name,
thanks!
No problem.
My lung capacity is
one hundred times that
of an Olympic diver, but
sure, try a giant hair
dryer.

It's not a hair
dryer. Not even Batman
has one of these!

Clearly he's
not missing
much.

Maybe
some alternative
energy?

Isn't it supposed to...turn?

We've tried everything. My science project and plans for a greener school are ruined.

And the crime rates in Metropolis are certainly going to go up. We're going to have to do some extra training.
I'll make night vision goggles!

I'm not ready to give up just yet.

Bumblebee, tell me everything you know about clouds.
Well...there are three primary ways that clouds dissipate.

One is an increase in temperature, two would be air sinking within the cloud, and the third is the clouds mixing with drier air--

Giant hair dryer for the win!
Yeah, but it didn't actually work.

Well, neither did your cold air.
Fair point.

I've got an even better idea!

JUST

Can you make some of those little beads that suck out moisture?
Silica gel? Sure, but how is that gonna...

You do the science and let me worry about the magic.

Aw, look— Babs left us a beacon. She's so sweet.

Did you create a solution?
I hope so.
We *know* so.

Esir dna enihs!

Please tell me these are environmentally friendly.
One hundred percent natural ***and*** organic, I promise.

Time for the cleanup.
Raeppasid!
Good work, team. The daylight has been saved.
All thanks to a combination of science and magic. You know, I think I might finally be getting the hang of this.

chapter six

drawn by Yancey Labat,
colored by Carrie Strachan

METROPOLIS HIGH SCHOOL

She's...cute.

I know she doesn't look like much, but she's super strong and super fast and a waaaaaaay better sidekick than Robin could ever be to Batman.

Watch!

Sing!

TWEETLE TWEET TWEET!
TWEEEEET! TWEET!
What are you trying to do, Babs? Annoy villains into submission?

It's a distraction technique!
She also has defense skills! Sparrow! Bird's nest!

Oh, well, now ***this*** is actually useful!
I know, right?

I think I've got a real shot at winning the science fair. Wanna take her out for a test spin?

Sure. But does she need to look so...robotic?
What do you mean?

I mean, I think she could use just a *little* more style.
Inim sbab!

Ohhhh! Okay, while you're at it, can I request a color change?
I think I know exactly what you have in mind.
Nibor!

Now you're speaking my language.
Perfect! Let's take this show on the road!

VROOOOM
Hello, Metropolis! We are ready to save you!

Old lady crossing the street!
Never fear, Sparrow is here!
Oh hey, great tag-line.

Thanks!
Sparrow, help!

You're welcome!

Help! Help!
What seems to be the problem?
MEW! MEW!
Oh Zatanna, I'm so glad you're here. My kitten is stuck in that tree!
This seems like a job for... **Sparrow!**

PURRR. PURR.

Thank you so much, little robot!
Her name's Sparrow! Don't forget it!

Ahhhhh!
This is literally a disaster!

What's wrong? Were you attacked? Was it Poison Ivy? Harley Quinn? *Ohhhh, the* ***Joker?***
No, it's worse!

Whaaaaa!
Just tell us what the trouble is and we'll take care of it.

Beatrice just texted me that Viv texted her that Auggie was going to text me to go to the movies with him but then my phone died before I even got to ask if this was like a heart emoji situation, or just a thumbs uppppppp...

Waaaaaahhhhh!
Oh, this *is* an emergency.

Grrrr...

Ta-da! Good as new!
Oh yeah, whatever. Thanks.
Gee, so glad we could help.

You should be proud, Babs. Sparrow is three for three in saving the day!
Yeah, I guess you're right.
It's all about marketing.

Presenting Batgirl's ***undefeated*** new sidekick! There has never been a foe with the ability to best the ***Sparrow!***

I must get this Batgirl to join my team.
Daily Planet
BATGIRL AND NEW SIDEKICK "SPARROW" SAVE METROPOLIS FROM LITERALLY EVERY VILLAIN
You rang.
Let's go kick some Bat-butt.
What about me?
Beep!
Beep!
Beep!
The Batmobile could use a wash.

What are we waiting for? My red-headed cousin and I just happen to be in the mood for some delicious burritos.

So...we meet again, my one true foe.

You may think you can defeat me, but you forget...

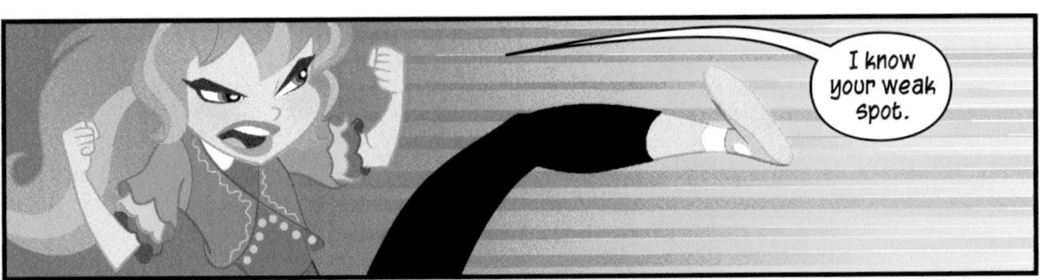
I know your weak spot.

THWACK
ICE

And *that's* what you do if the soda machine goes on the fritz.
Seems... excessive. And honestly, Babs, if *I'M* saying that, you might want to rethink your strategy.
ICE

You know, I have no idea who this young woman is, but service like that deserves a raise.

Something fishy is going on.

Well, today's special *is* mahi-mahi tacos!

I'm heading into my office to do paperwork. But I've got my eyes on you, Gordon.

Phew! Great cover, Zee.
I know.

Time to get to work!

I'd like a burrito but on corn tortillas instead of flour, extra guacamole, but no avocado, hold the cheese, extra beans, and salsa but with just the tomatoes, pick out all the onions—
Uhhh...she's training today. How about a quesadilla?

First we'll test balance...

ZZZWIPPP

Then agility...
Incredible service!
Wow!
PICK UP

And finally, stamina...

Holy guacamole! I think she's got it!
Holy guacamole indeed.

Dr. Sieve!
I'm thrilled to see my lunch break comes with a science fair preview. Great work, Ms....?

Gordon. Barbara Gordon. And that soon-to-be award-winning invention is Sparrow. How about some fish tacos on the house?

Fish tacos sound delightful. And Ms. Zatara, I'm very glad to see our little chat seems to have paid off.
Oh absolutely. I'm learning a lot from Babs. It's like inspiration overdrive.

Overdrive! Overdrive!
Oh no, I didn't mean—!

Sparrow! No! Stop!

Okay, I can fix this...

Ton os tsaf doof!

Wow, gravity is super weird today, huh? Ha, ha...heh.

Thanks for the assist.
I mean, this one was kind of my fault.

I didn't tell you the command words. How would you have known? Anyway, everything's fine.
Sparrow, get Zee a large lemon-lime soda.

CLICK! CLICK!

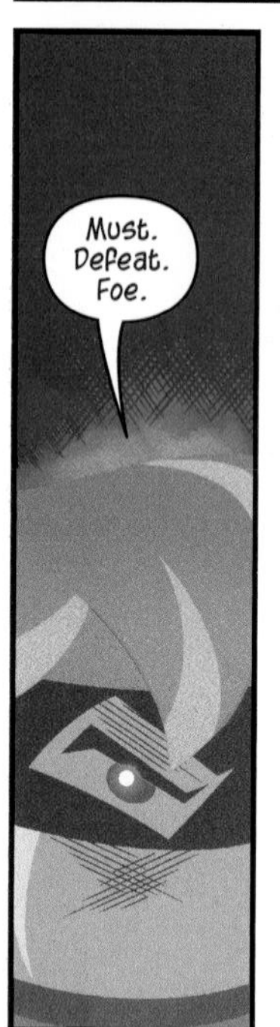
Must. Defeat. Foe.

CRACK!!
Sparrow! *No!*

Sparrow!

I'm calling in backup.
SHG GROUP TEXT

I think I've got it under control.

Gordon!

Are you **attacking** a customer?!

This is the last straw, Gordon!

Excuse me, sir. Could I get a little more guacamole?

I'm a little busy at the—

I do believe the customer is ***always*** right. I'd hate to have to leave you a bad ***Welp*** review.

By the way, we are so lucky your employee knows the Heimlich maneuver. If Barbara hadn't just jumped on her, my cousin would have ***choked!***

You should probably give that girl a raise.

chapter seven

PART 1
drawn and colored by Emma Kubert

PART 2
drawn and colored by Erich Owen

Sweet JUSTICE
SHOES
SHAKES MALTS
CANDY COOKIES
MENU
Sweet JUSTICE
CLEANER
Hi, Barry, one mint chocolate...
Here you are, Zee!
...chip cone please. Wow, you're fast.

I'm so glad you called this meeting, Diana. I finally think I've figured out my science project. But don't worry, I am still available to help with anything any of you need!
Actually, that is *exactly* why I called the meeting.
To talk about my project?
To talk about your *help.*
What does that mean?
It's just...what Kara's trying to say is...
Sparrow's microchip was missing after she left the Burrito Bucket.
Babs, you don't honestly think I'm *stealing?!*

No one thinks you are doing anything on purpose.
It's just...
Thank you, Jessica.
Whenever things go wrong you just happen to be there.
I would never do **anything** to ruin your projects! I can't believe you think I would.
Mine's not ruined.
Actually, after our disaster I decided to go big instead. I built a giant honeycomb display with real honey.
I think it's even better!
That's great, Karen. Let me know if you want any more help with it.

No, the helping must cease. You have shattered the camel's spinal cord with strands of hay.
You don't want me around?
I'd never do anything to sabotage any of you. There's got to be something sinister behind this...
What if someone is setting me up? Karen, you still believe me, right?
It's just until after the science fair.
Well, fine. I'm better as a solo act anyway.
Tixe egats tfel!
Whew, that could have been really awkward.

METROPOLIS

Dnif ym wodahs!

SWEET JUSTIC

SENRE VILLE

So...whoever this is has been following me since the very beginning.
SMALLVILLE
SWEET JUSTICE
SENRE VILLE
Oh, hello again!
Uh... h-hi?
Welcome to SMALLVILLE
I knew someone had to have stolen that fertilizer!
SMALLVILLE
METROPOLIS
METROPOLIS HIGH
SENRE VILLE

Not much of a trace here.
Okay, to be fair, that failure was probably on me. Though Diana's makeover **did** look fabulous.
Wait, that doesn't look right.
Someone is stealing Jessica's solar panels!
And if I text her...they'll all blame me.
SMALLVILLE
HIGH
CENTRAL BUSINESS DISTRICT
SWEET JUSTICE

That explains Sparrow's missing microchip. Now to finally see where this ends...
BURRITO BUCKET
Metropolis High? I was just there.
METROPOLIS
METROPOLIS HIGH
SMALLVILLE
There's no way this can be right. Sparrow was the last project I worked on.
Fine. I'll check it out just in case.
SWEET JUSTICE
♫♪La, la, la♪♫
I'm just an ordinary student heading into school on a Saturday? Sure.

The storage room?
METROPOLIS HIGH SCHOOL
It's kinda creepy being here when no one else is around...

Wait, this doesn't make any sense.
TEMPORARY OFFICE OF VISITING INSTRUCTOR AND SCIENCE FAIR JUDGE
DR. PENELOPE SIEVE
project CADMUS

Kcolnu eht hturt!

Gasp!
Kara will *have* to believe me now!
CLICK
CLICK
Karen's new model?! I haven't even gone near it!
Yes, but you were such a help in leading me to students with the most advanced projects.
You have excellent taste.
Dr. Sieve! I don't understand. What are you doing?
TEMPORARY OFFICE OF VISITING INSTRUCTOR AND SCIENCE FAIR JUDGE DR. PENELOPE SIEVE Project CADMUS
Oh, Ms. Zatara, it's a shame you won't be around long enough to find out.

Dr. Sieve? You—you're **stealing** everyone's projects.
You say stealing, Zee. I say making a few improvements to some interesting projects I've been working on for months.
And it's very sweet how my work has inspired the students here at Metropolis High.

They weren't **inspired** by your work. They came up with these projects on their own!
It's the word of a high school student versus a world-renowned scientist.
Or rather, it would be, if I let you go.

Sparrow!

Not quite.
Hey!

I'm calling this a Sieve-bot. I've made a few improvements.
ZZZZZAP!
ZZZZZZZAP!!
You won't get away with this.
Oh, I've been getting away with it for my entire career. I don't intend to stop now.
Sigh.
Why? What about that whole story you told me about learning to work with others?

Precisely. I've learned the easiest way to get ahead is to let others do the dangerous work—and then take the credit.

For example, the simplest way for me to find the best and brightest minds at Metropolis High was to follow you around while you floundered.
And you did beautifully. I owe you one.

I *trusted* you.
Yes, well. Seems like you finally learned something valuable. Never trust anyone.

Sieve-bot, keep an eye on the captive while I go figure out what to do with our little problem.

Evael eht
tsen!

Dnif ym
enohp!

!!!!!!!!!
TAP
TAP

Zatanna!

After all you've put us through, this better be—

—good. Wait, is that my fertilizer?
Dr. Sieve was behind it all, Supergirl, not me.

SPARROW!
It's not her, Batgirl! Be careful!

Great thinking, Green Lantern.

No more chip, no more problem!

It seems we owe you an apology, Zee.

Yes, it appears we have all placed our battle sandals into our oral cavities. We are truly sorry.
You're about to be more than ***sorry***, Wonder Woman.

Just return the experiments to their rightful owners and no one has to get hurt.
Oh, someone is definitely going to get hurt.
DR. PENELOPE SIEVE
Project CADMUS
I couldn't agree more.
BOOM!

WOOOSH

The honeycomb!
Oh! Great idea.

As much as I hate to take out aggression on a fellow scientist... I'm not sorry about this!
Aw, Bumblebee, I'm so proud.
I'll squash you like a bug!

And now...

...just a bit of centrifugal force!

You paid attention!

And a bit of wind power to make the honey stickier!

Aww, Zatanna. I can't believe you remembered that.
WOOOSH

It turns out science is pretty useful after all.
The police are on their way!

I guess we better get these projects back to their rightful owners before the science fair.
But who will be the judge now?
Wait. Does this mean no Cadmus internship?
Maybe not, but isn't the real prize all the science we learned along the way?
Who *are* you?
Maybe that fertilizer helps with personal growth, too. Just...please don't make me touch it.

chapter eight

drawn and colored
by Erich Owen

Zee! Over here!
METROPOLIS HI
SCIENCE FAI

Wow, Barry, I had no idea you were into cooking.
Oh, actually it was the slow part I thought would be a challenge.
The Effects of Slow Cooking on Nutritional Content

Hey, Jessica.
OPTIMAL DISPLAY PRESENTATION OF VARIOUS SPORTS TROPHIES
I cannot believe you, Hal Jordan.
The arrogance, the extreme ego of making an entire project about your own physical prowess!
So, you've noticed my physical prowess?

PREVIOUS WINNERS GALLERY
The Preservation of Ancient Artifacts in Controlled Temperature Environments

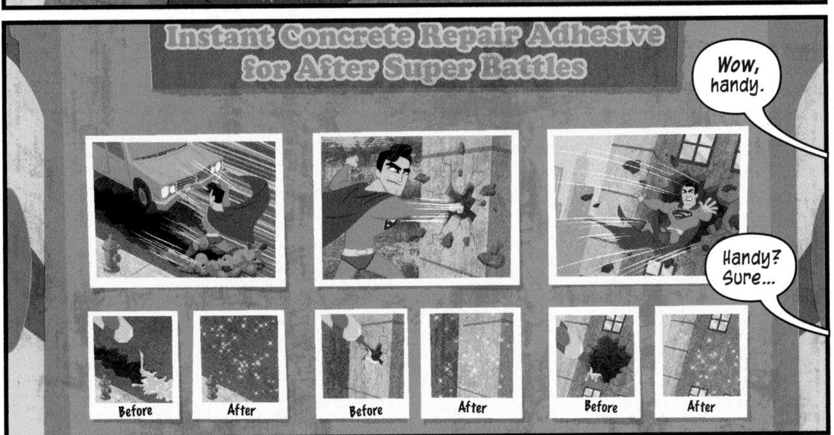
Instant Concrete Repair Adhesive for After Super Battles
Wow, handy.
Handy? Sure...
Before
After
Before
After
Before
After

WOOOSH!
...but it lacks pizzazz.

And vision.

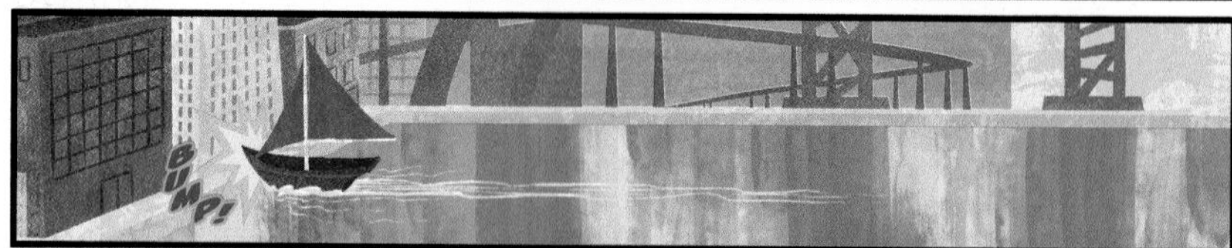
BUMP!

A Rube Goldberg machine?

The Rube Goldberg machine.

Of course, I've changed the dolls a bit since my win. It used to be a tiny Superman, but I like to keep up with the times.

Lex Luthor. If anyone would show up years later to gloat about a science fair win, it's you.
Being proud of our superior intellect is a Luthor family trait. Much as I suppose all style and no substance is a Zatara family trait.

Etib ruoy—
Hi! Zee! Do you need any help setting up? I'm so excited to see what you did for your project.

You got lucky this time, Luthor!

I'm so excited! **Clearly,** Sparrow is winning material if Dr. Sieve went out of her way to duplicate her.
You've done amazing work.
Thanks for the hair. It's the perfect touch.
SPARROW!

BEEZ BUZZ
SPARROW!
And now—

Oh! I didn't know you made a backup.

SCIENCE FAIR
I didn't.

Sieve-bots!
Dr. Sieve must have made duplicates!
Um, this is more than duplicates...this is an entire army.
EXIT

AHHH!

You'll pay for that! Only LexCorp bots are allowed to sabotage...I mean, not that they ever would.

There's a janitor's closet just behind us for a quick change.

Let's take out these impostors.

OOF!
Okay, I was already angry, but being captured by my own design is *infuriating!*

They're too strong to penetrate.
I know! I'm so sorry that I'm so good at this!
EXIT
EXIT

Evael eht tsen.

Get away from her, bot!
No! Wait!

That's Sparrow!
Oh, right, the one with the hair. Sorry.

I can take these out one at a time, but it'll take forever!

Wait! I have an idea. Sparrow—**sing!**

TWEEDLE TWEEDLE TWEET! TWEETLE TWEET TWEET! TWEEEEET!
Oh no, why would you want to make things worse?!

TWEEDLE TWEEDLE TWEET!

TWEETLE TWEET! TWEET TWEET! TWEEEEET!

TWEET! TWEETLE TWEET TWEET!

It's working!
Told ya!
TWEEDLE TWEEDLE TWEET! TWEETLE TWEET TWEET! TWEEEEET!

WHIRRR

CLICK!

Great work, team! Batgirl, I am very impressed with how you kept a chilly head.
Now let's get our science fair on!

Obviously, we no longer have a guest judge. Today dissolved into so much chaos I didn't really want to give an award.
That's not fair!
Groan!
SPARROW!

But the school board has informed me that it's a breach of our funding if I don't. So congrats to—
Ohmigosh, I did it!
After what those robots did to the school? I think not, Ms. Gordon.
SPARROW!

Today's winner is Zee Zatara and her cloud evaporation concoction. You'll be pleased to know Cadmus is very interested in purchasing the patent...
Actually, the prize and the Cadmus internship should really go to Karen. It was her experiment. I just helped.

I don't really care. Whatever lets us keep our science funding and will pay for a janitor to come clean up this mess.

Zee, you didn't have to do that! The solution was your idea!
I know! But you created it and you'll enjoy the internship way more than I would. Even if I *do* kinda love science now.
You do?
Sure. It turns out science is just like being part of a superhero team—when you combine the right elements, it's magic.
ZATANNA?!
Ugh, plus there's the downside of magic...
What's that?
Magic isn't always an exact science.

METROPOLIS HIGH SCHOOL

Amanda Deibert is an award-winning television and comic book writer. Her work includes *DC Super Hero Girls, Teen Titans Go!, Wonder Woman '77, Sensation Comics Featuring Wonder Woman*, and a story in *Love Is Love* (a *New York Times* #1 bestseller) along with comics for IDW, Dark Horse, Bedside Press, and Storm King. She's written TV shows for CBS, Syfy, OWN, Hulu, and former vice president Al Gore's international climate broadcast, *24 Hours of Reality*.

Yancey Labat is the bestselling illustrator of the original *DC Super Hero Girls* graphic novel series. He got his start at Marvel Comics before moving on to illustrate children's books from *Hello Kitty* to *Peanuts* for Scholastic, as well as books for Chronicle Books, ABC Mouse, and others. His book *How Many Jelly Beans?* with writer Andrea Menotti won the 2013 Cook Prize for best STEM (Science, Technology, Education, Math) picture book from Bank Street College of Education.

Erich Owen is a cartoonist living in San Diego. His first graphic novel series, *Mail Order Ninja*, which he co-created and illustrated, was published in 2005. Since then, he's been drawing all kinds of comic book projects! Currently, he draws *Teen Titans Go!* and *DC Super Hero Girls* for DC Comics.

Marcelo DiChiara, a Brazilian artist, began his career doing illustrations for French publisher Semic. In the United States, he has worked for Image Comics and Marvel Comics on *Iron Man & Power Pack, Marvel Adventures Super Heroes*, and Marvel Super Hero Squad. Since 2014, he has worked for DC Comics as an artist on *Smallville, Bombshells United, DC Super Hero Girls*, and *Teen Titans Go!*

Agnes Garbowska has made her name in comics illustrating such titles as the *New York Times* bestselling and award-winning *DC Super Hero Girls* for DC Comics. In addition, her portfolio includes a long run on *My Little Pony* for IDW, *Teen Titans Go!* for DC Comics, *Grumpy Cat* for Dynamite Entertainment, and *Sonic Universe* "Off Panel" strips for Archie Comics.

Sarah Leuver is a comic and storyboard artist who has worked for IDW, DC Comics, and Aerial Contrivance Workshop. She loves dogs and superheroes, and lives in the Bay Area with her own dog, Oliver. (He is not a superhero, but he *does* have a cape.)

Emma Kubert is a young and talented artist who has worked for various companies including Image Comics, Dynamite Entertainment, and, of course, DC Comics, where she's contributed to *DC Super Hero Girls: Weird Science* and *Teen Titans Go!* She is drawn to stories with funny, strong female characters, which made working on *DC Super Hero Girls* a dream come true. She is currently working with fellow artist Rusty Gladd on their creator-owned project *Inkblot* for Image Comics, which will be published in 2020.

Carrie Strachan is an award-awaiting colorist who has worked on *Hellblazer*, *Smallville: Season 11*, *MAD Magazine*, and *MAD Spy vs. Spy: An Explosive Celebration*. She currently lives in San Diego with her husband, Matt, where she's hard at work on more DC Super Hero Girls.

Wendy Broome, colorist extraordinaire, has been coloring comics since the dawn of time... well the dawn of Photoshop anyway. Over the years she has worked on everything from *DV8* to *Astro City* and *DC Comics Bombshells*, but she's having fun with the DC Super Hero Girls and *Teen Titans Go!* stories in her current workload. Her children, Jaedon and Camryn, only wish she'd started coloring comics like these years ago so they would have been allowed to read them in elementary school.

Silvana Brys is a colorist and graphic designer who has colored *Scooby-Doo, Where Are You?*, *Teen Titans Go!*, *Scooby-Doo Team-Up*, and *Looney Tunes* for DC Comics, plus *Tom & Jerry* and many other comics and books. She lives in a small village in Argentina. Her home is also her office and she loves to create there, surrounded by forests and mountains.

Who comes out on top when a Bumblebee, a journalist, and a super-villain fight?

THE NEW YORK TIMES BESTSELLING
DC
Super Hero Girls
BASED ON THE HIT ANIMATED SERIES!
A+
MIDTERMS
A GRAPHIC NOVEL
WRITTEN BY AMY WOLFRAM
ILLUSTRATED BY YANCEY LABAT

top the leader board
gh and the upcoming midterms
who's the best in class...unless a certain funny
y!

d Yancey Labat welcome you back to Metropolis High
the worst part of the year: midterm exams.

See you in Fall 2020!

Looks like we're the first ones here. We've got the scoop!

Are you ready?
Composing the perfect shot takes time.

You're out of time! They're coming!

My camera!
WHOOSH

Get out of my way!
MAERC GNIVAHS!
Get a grip!
Whoa!
Thank you, Zatanna!
CRASH
Ungh.

This will teach you not to steal.
No it won't, Wonder Woman.

Learn some manners!
POLICE

Phltttttt.

Phltttttt.

We came. We saw. We kicked some butt!
Let's go eat. I'm **starving.**

I just need a few more photos.

We've only got 45 minutes before school starts, Lois!
That's just enough time to write the cover story and post the newspaper before morning bell!

And I know just the angle.

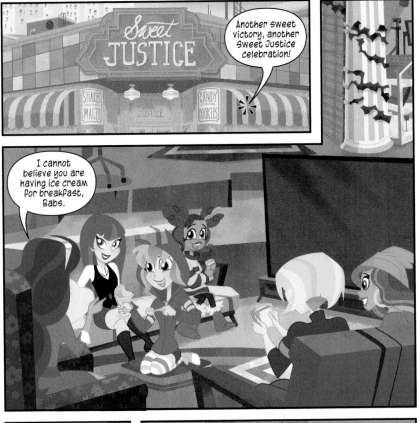

Sweet JUSTICE
SHAKES MALTS
CANDY COOKIES
Another sweet victory, another Sweet Justice celebration!

I cannot believe you are having ice cream for breakfast, Babs.

What? It's the most important meal of the day.

SUPER HERO GIRLS OR SUPER DISASTER?

To be continued in
DC Super Hero Girls: Midterms
in stores September 2020!

Lois Lane is prepared for the best summer of all time—her new sure-to-go-viral video channel, her best friend Kristen, and their town's fireworks celebration are all coming together perfectly. But when things fall apart, Lois doubles down on her efforts for fame, testing her friendship in ways she couldn't imagine.

NEW YORK TIMES BESTSELLING CO-AUTHOR OF LUMBERJANES

GRACE ELLIS

LOIS LANE and the FRIENDSHIP CHALLENGE

illustrated by BRITTNEY WILLIAMS

Grace Ellis and **Brittney Williams**
will prepare Lois (and you!) for the confusing
worlds of social media and friendship in summer 2020!

1,000,000,000
1,000,000,000
Okay, so first thing of all, I have a perfect plan for how
LOIS! CAMERA! ACTION!
is gonna go viral on VidMe.
views
views
views
views
ViDoMe
Lois! Camera! Action!
"Like always, Kristen and I will celebrate our friend-iversary during the fireworks after the jamboree bike race, and we'll make it into a #FriendshipChallenge video that captures the hearts of the whole entire planet."
Actually, I won't be here for the fireworks this—
And then next—
We become the youngest VidMers to get 10 million subscribers.
HOME
Channel
New
Inbox
•Settings
•Help
"Which, it's like, I know Lottie Live already has that many, but she's already 14, and we're only 13, so we win! And then Lottie Live cries but also we're best friends with her because of doing the #FriendshipChallenge."
I'm best friends with Lois Lane!
Lottie LIVE
Bff

"And then everyone has to listen to us and know all about our friendship.
VidMe
"Easy peasy.
"Best summer ever."
So I woke up early for nothing?
No! Listen!
VidMe is the first draft of history! We have important things to say, and the whole world should hear them!
It sounds like you should be doing journalism.
Like "the first draft of history" is literally journalism.
No! What do you even know?!
VidMe

I'm interning this summer with the *Liberty View Daily Patriot*, so I'm basically a professional journalist now.
So.
I know some things.
Oh yeah?

What super important thing are you journalism-ing for that toilet paper?
First thing of all, rude.

Second, I'm investigating a local government agency's recent release of several wards of the state.

She's doing a story about dog adoptions at the animal shelter.
Ruff Life

Hey!
Hey yourself, man, I'll call out anyone.

People rely on the news to tell them what's happening in their community, including animal-related news, which is ***news.***
You want the news? I'll show you what's news.

Breaking news: Look at this beautiful angel. Look at her!

You two should come by the *Daily Patriot* offices! It would be so fun. You can see my desk! I put knickknacks on it!
I would, but I'm swamped this week.
HONK HONK!

I'm leaving for sleepaway camp right after the jamboree—
Hey!
Who's that over there?
To be continued in
Lois Lane and the Friendship Challenge
in stores Summer 2020!

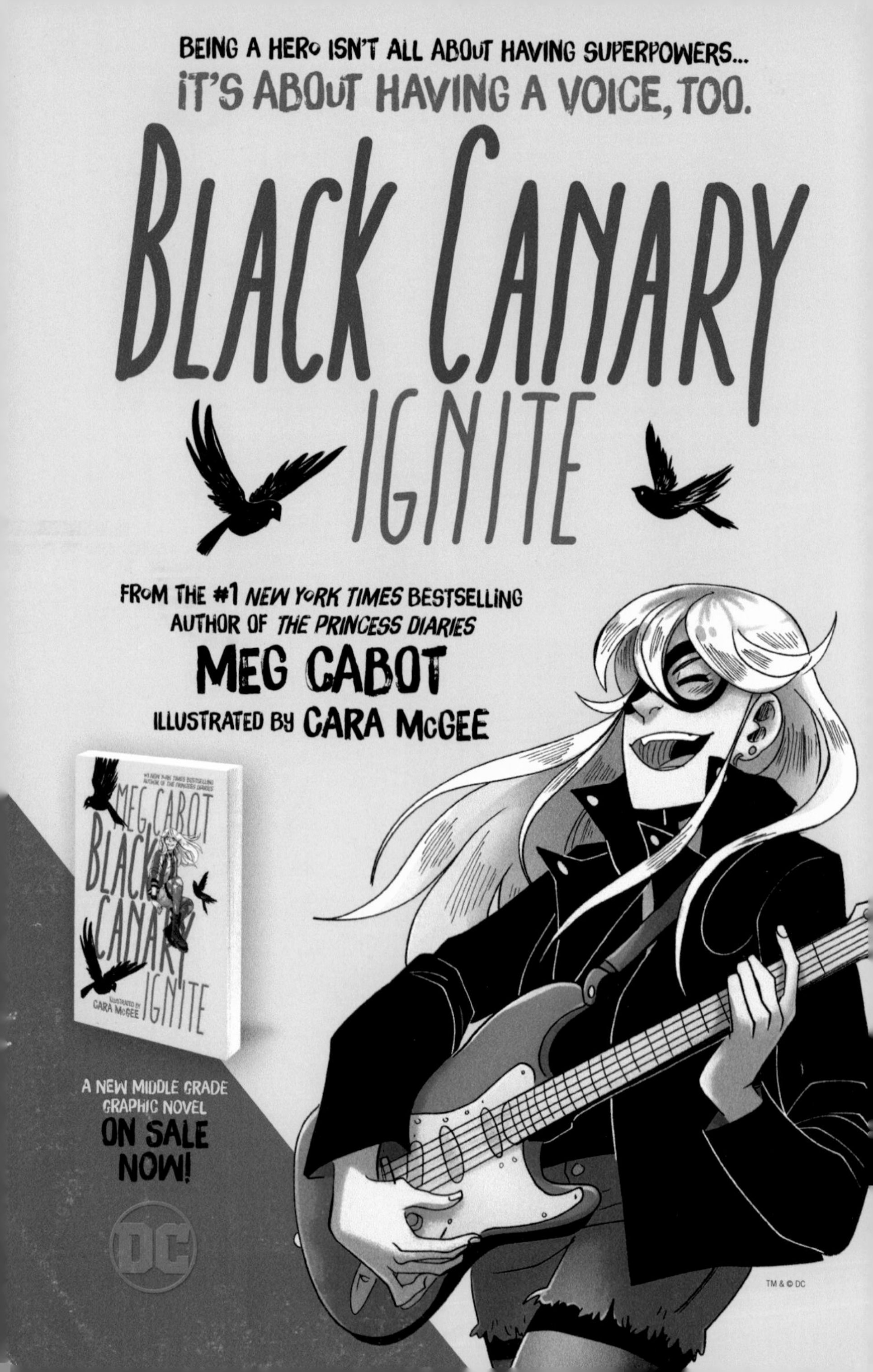